This Little Tiger book belongs to:

_____

_____

_____

_____

For Deborah
~ D B

For Noah who is little, and
for Jake who wants to be BIG
~ J C

LITTLE TIGER PRESS
An imprint of Magi Publications
1 The Coda Centre, 189 Munster Road, London SW6 6AW
www.littletigerpress.com
First published in Great Britain 2001
This edition published 2006
Text copyright © David Bedford 2001, 2006
Illustrations copyright © Jane Chapman 2001, 2006
David Bedford and Jane Chapman have asserted their rights to be
identified as the author and illustrator of this work under the
Copyright, Designs and Patents Act, 1988.
Printed in China • All rights reserved
ISBN-13: 978-1-84506-362-7 • ISBN-10: 1-84506-362-7
1 3 5 7 9 10 8 6 4 2

Big Bear
Little Bear

David Bedford   Jane Chapman

LITTLE TIGER PRESS
London

One bright cold morning Little Bear helped Mother Bear scoop snow out of their den.

"This will make more room for you to play," said Mother Bear. "You're getting bigger now."

"I want to be as big as you when I'm grown up," said Little Bear. He stretched up his arms and made himself as big as he could.

Mother Bear stretched to the sky.
"You'll have to eat and eat to be
as big as I am," she said.
"When I'm big, I'll wrestle you in
the snow," said Little Bear. Wrestling
in the snow was his favourite game.

"You're not big enough to wrestle me yet," said Mother Bear, laughing.

She rolled Little Bear over and over in the soft snow and he giggled.

"When I'm grown up I want to run as fast as you, Mummy," he said.

"You'll have to practise if you want to be as fast as I am," said Mother Bear.

Little Bear darted away and
ran as fast as he could . . .

but Mother Bear quickly passed him, calling, "Run faster!"

"I can't," said Little Bear. "I'm not grown up yet."

"I'll show you what it's like to be grown up," said Mother Bear. "Climb on to my shoulders!"

When Little Bear stood on his mother's shoulders he could see to the end of the world, and when he reached up his hands he could nearly touch the sky.

"Now you *are* big," said Mother Bear.

"Let's run," cried Mother Bear. She ran
faster and faster, so that Little Bear felt
the wind rushing against his face and
blowing his ears back.

Suddenly, Mother Bear leapt into the air.
Little Bear saw the world rushing under him.
"I'm flying like a bird," he shouted. Then
he saw where they were going to land . . .

...*SPLASH!*

Mother Bear dived into the cold water. "This is how you'll swim when you're grown up," she said.

Little Bear watched his mother carefully so he would know what to do next time.

"I'll soon be able to swim like that," he told himself.

Mother Bear climbed out of the water with Little Bear still clinging tightly to her back.

"Will I *really* be as big as you when I'm grown up?" asked Little Bear.

"Yes you will," said his mother, "but I don't want you to grow up yet."

"Why not?" asked Little Bear.

"You won't be able to sit on my shoulders when you're grown up," said Mother Bear, as she carried Little Bear back to their snow den.

Little Bear was tired after wrestling, running, flying and swimming.

"You can still cuddle me when I'm grown up," he said, sleepily. "But Mummy, I don't want to grow up yet."

"That's good," said Mother Bear,
holding him close, "because . . .

"... you're perfect just the way you are."

Little Bear snuggled into his mother's soft fur, and they went to sleep together in their cosy den in the snow.

More magical books from Little Tiger Press

The Snow Angel
Christine Leeson · Jane Chapman

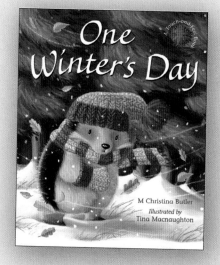

One Winter's Day
M Christina Butler
Illustrated by Tina Macnaughton

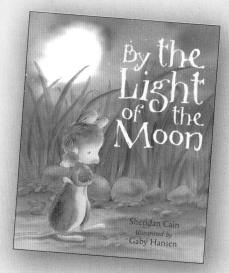

By the Light of the Moon
Sheridan Cain
Illustrated by Gaby Hansen

The Very Snowy Christmas
Diana Hendry · Jane Chapman

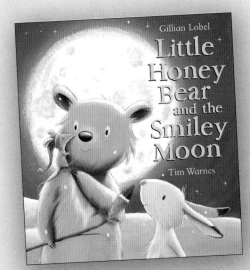

Gillian Lobel
Little Honey Bear and the Smiley Moon
Tim Warnes

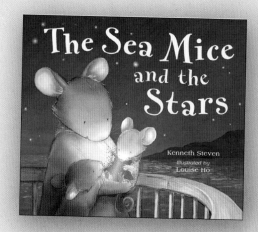

The Sea Mice and the Stars
Kenneth Steven
Illustrated by Louise Ho

For information regarding any of the above titles or for our catalogue, please contact us:
Little Tiger Press, 1 The Coda Centre, 189 Munster Road, London SW6 6AW
Tel: 020 7385 6333 Fax: 020 7385 7333
E-mail: info@littletiger.co.uk www.littletigerpress.com